10/10

PLEASE WRITE BACK!

To Charlie
—J.M.

Text and illustrations copyright © 2010 by Jennifer E. Morris.

Library of Congress Cataloging-in-Publication Data
Morris, J. E. (Jennifer E.)
Please write back! / by Jennifer E. Morris.
p. cm. -- (Scholastic reader. Level 1)
Summary: Alfie writes a letter to his grandmother and eagerly
awaits her reply.
ISBN-13: 978-0-545-11506-3 (pbk. : alk. paper)
ISBN-10: 0-545-11506-X (pbk. : alk. paper)
[1. Letters--Fiction. 2. Grandmothers--Fiction.] I. Title. II. Series.

PZ7.M82824Ple 2010
[E]--dc22   2009011176

ISBN: 978-0-545-11506-3

10 9 8 7 6 5 4 3 2   10 11 12 13 14/0
Printed in the U.S.A. 40 • First printing, April 2010

PLEASE WRITE BACK!

SCHOLASTIC READER
LEVEL 1
50-250 WORDS

by Jennifer E. Morris

Cartwheel
·B·O·O·K·S·®

SCHOLASTIC INC.
New York Toronto London Auckland
Sydney Mexico City New Delhi Hong Kong

Alfie wrote a letter to
Grandma.

Alfie addressed the letter.

He stamped the letter.

And he mailed the letter.

Then he waited for
Grandma to write back.

He waited the next day.

And the next day.

And the next day.

But Grandma's letter
did not come.

The next day, Alfie
did not wait for the mail.

"Are you Alfie?" asked
the mailman.

"Do you have a letter for me?" asked Alfie.

"No," said the mailman.

"I have a box."

Inside was a letter.

Dear Alfie,

I love you too!

Love,
Grandma

And a big batch of cookies!
Hooray!

Dear Grandma,

Thank you for
the cookies!

Love,
Alfie